Toot & Puddle

I'll Be Home for Christmas

by Holly Hobbie

LITTLE, BROWN AND COMPANY
Books for Young Readers
New York   Boston

Little, Brown and Company

Hachette Book Group USA
237 Park Avenue, New York, NY 10017
Visit our Web site at www.lb-kids.com

First Paperback Edition: October 2008
First published in hardcover in 2001 by Little, Brown and Company

Library of Congress Cataloging-in-Publication Data
Hobbie, Holly.
   Toot & Puddle: I'll be home for Christmas/ by Holly Hobbie—1st ed.
      p. cm.
Summary: Delayed by a snowstorm, Toot gets unexpected help getting back to Woodcock Pocket in time to celebrate Christmas with Puddle.
   ISBN 978-0-316-36623-6 (hc) / ISBN 978-0-316-03383-1 (pb)
      [1. Christmas—Fiction. 2. Blizzards—Fiction. 3. Pigs—Fiction. I. Title: Toot and Puddle. II. Title.
PZ7.H6517 Toc 2001
[E]—dc21   00-042816

10 9 8 7 6 5 4 3 2 1

TWP

Printed in Singapore

The paintings for this book were done in watercolor.
The text was set in Optima, and the display types are Windsor Light and Poetica.
The title type was handlettered.

To Hope

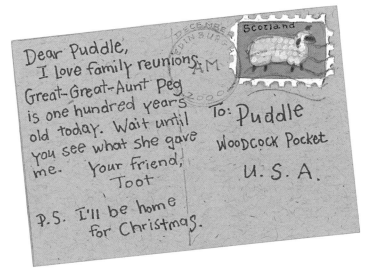

Dear Puddle,
   I love family reunions.
Great-Great-Aunt Peg
is one hundred years
old today. Wait until
you see what she gave
me.   Your Friend,
        Toot

P.S. I'll be home
    for Christmas.

To: Puddle
Woodcock Pocket

U. S. A.

Scotland

DECEMBER
EDINBURG
AM
2000

"My dear Toot," said the ancient aunt, "this is for you.
It is my lucky nut!"

Back in Woodcock Pocket, Puddle couldn't wait for Toot any longer. Christmas was only a few days away. And there was everything to do.

Puddle signed all the cards *Merry Christmas!* *and Puddle*
He would have to wait until Toot returned before he could mail them.

To: puddle@woodcockpocket.com
Subject: Christmas

Puds,

Edinburgh is having an ice storm. All
flights delayed. But don't decorate the
tree without me. I'm on my way
home...somehow.

Your pal,

Toot

P.S. I'm full of Christmas spirit.

Meanwhile…
at Woodcock Pocket

"Fruitcake is one of Toot's favorite things," said Puddle.

"How many do you think we need?" Tulip asked.

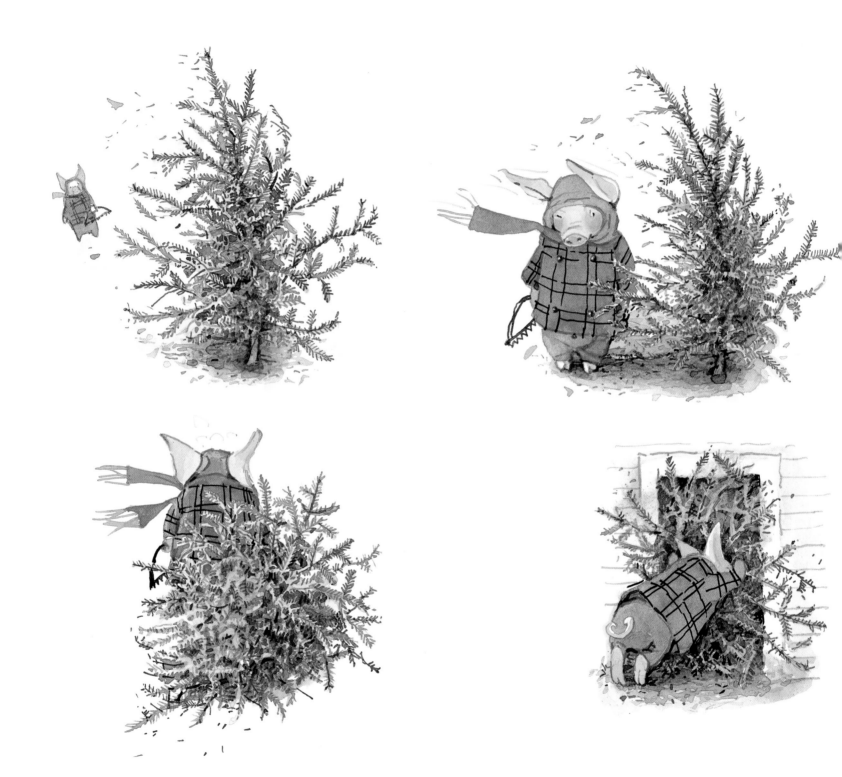

Christmas Eve was only one day away.
"How can Toot possibly get home in time?" Puddle said.
"He has to," said Tulip.

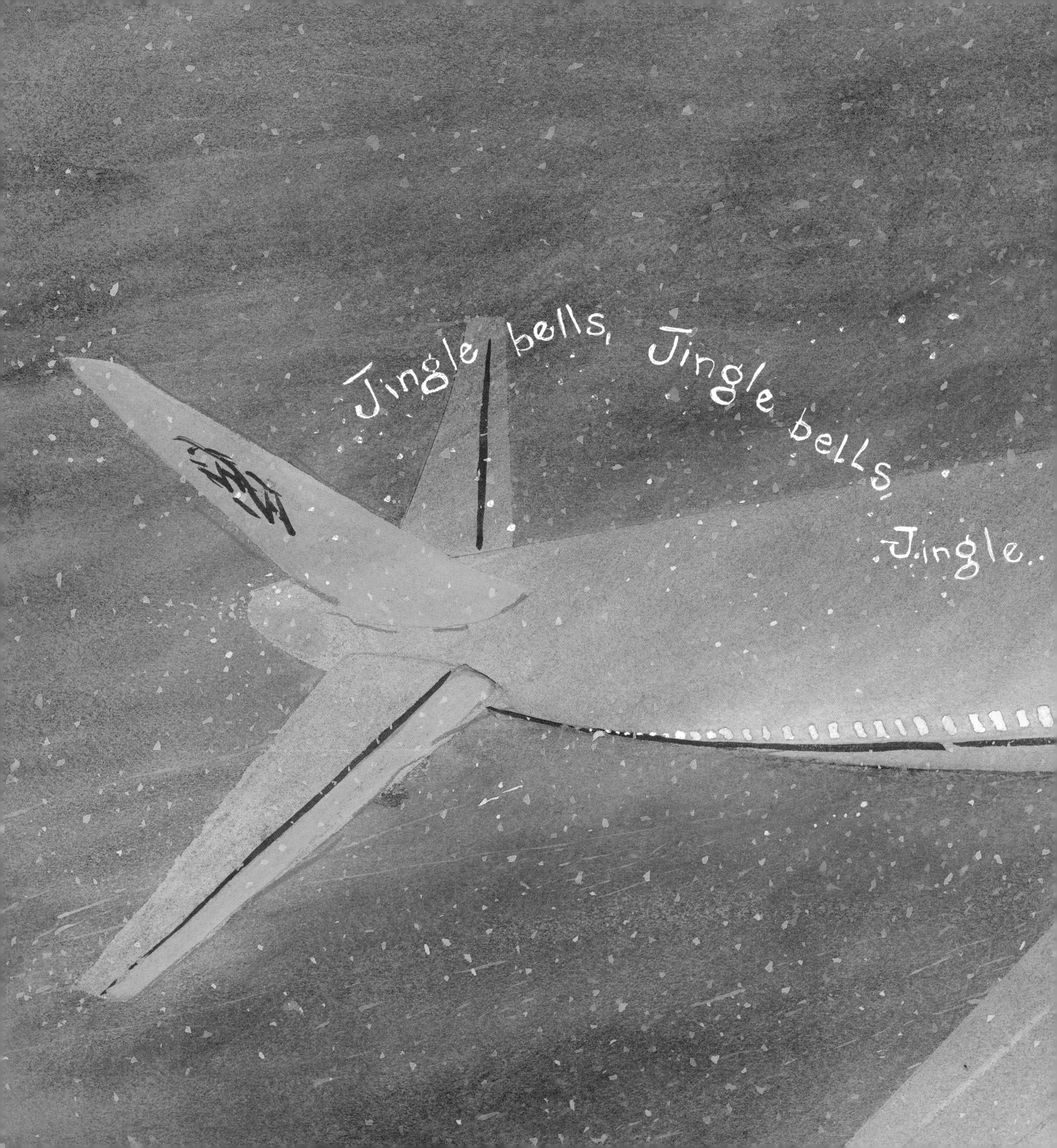
Jingle bells, Jingle bells,
Jingle..

all the way...

WIDE WORLD AIRWAYS

When Toot finally arrived in Boston, it was snowing and very late.
Everything had come to a stop, even trains and buses and taxicabs.
I promised Puddle I'd be home tonight, Toot thought.

Toot hiked far from the city. The night was cold and the snow was deep. He trudged on until, at last, he could go no further.

Toot hugged himself to keep warm. There in his pocket he felt the lucky nut. He'd forgotten all about that special gift. *It's Christmas Eve,* he thought. *I wish I was home in Woodcock Pocket.*

"It's snowing so hard," Puddle said.
"It's beautiful," said Tulip.

"If only Toot were here."

Toot was startled by a tinkling, jingling sound.
As he peered into the dark, he saw a faint light coming
toward him. It twinkled and flickered in the snowy night.

"Where are you headed, laddie?"
"Woodcock Pocket," said Toot. "It's miles and miles from here."
"Climb aboard," the driver said. "I know the way."

The first snowfall had turned Woodcock Pocket into a sparkling
wonderland. Everything was ready. Everything was perfect.
But where was his friend?

Then…
"I'm home!"
"You are! You're finally here!"

Toot told his friends of his adventure and how he finally got back to Woodcock Pocket.
"I loved the sleigh ride," he said. "It felt like we were flying."
"I wonder who that driver was," said Puddle.

"Let's hang this on the tree," said Toot.

"What is that?" Tulip asked.

"It's beautiful," said Puddle.

"This is Great-Great-Aunt Peg's lucky nut," Toot told them.

It wasn't easy to fall asleep on Christmas Eve.
"Toot," Puddle said, "do you hear a jingling sound?"
Toot listened. "Maybe."
"I think I definitely hear something," said Puddle.
"Then I think we'd better go to sleep," Toot said. "Right away."
Puddle agreed. "I'll count to twenty."
But before Puddle counted to ten, he and his friend were fast asleep.

When they wake up, it will be Christmas.